Shhh!
The Baby's Asleep

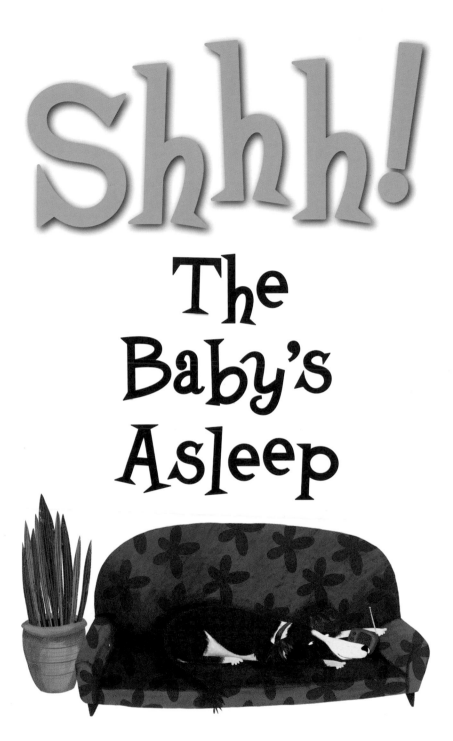

For Vivian and Isaac.—J. B.-W.

For all noisy families of the world.
And especially to my son, J, and my niece, Lu.—E

Published by Charlesbridge
9 Galen Street
Watertown, MA 02472
(617) 926-0329
www.charlesbridge.com

Library of Congress Cataloging-in-Publication Data
Names: Brown-Wood, JaNay, author. | Elissambura, illustrator.
Title: Shhh! The baby's asleep / JaNay Brown-Wood; illustrated by Elissambura.
Description: Watertown, MA : Charlesbridge, 2021. | Audience: Ages 2-5. |
Summary: Baby is finally asleep as Mom begins to shush the rest of the family; but when they are
  all finally quiet, baby wakes up and big brother realizes just what baby needs—a book!
Identifiers: LCCN 2019035069 (print) | LCCN 2019035070 (ebook) | ISBN 9781580895224 (hardcover) |
  ISBN 9781632898197 (ebook)
Subjects: LCSH: Infants—Juvenile fiction. | Families—Juvenile fiction. | Sleep—Juvenile fiction. |
  Noise—Juvenile fiction. | Humorous stories. | CYAC: Stories in rhyme. | Babies—Fiction. |
  Family life—Fiction. | Sleep—Fiction. | Noise—Fiction. | African Americans—Fiction. |
  Humorous stories. | LCGFT: Humorous fiction. | Picture books.
Classification: LCC PZ8.3.B81577 Sh 2021 (print) | LCC PZ8.3.B81577 (ebook) | DDC [E]—dc23
LC record available at https://lccn.loc.gov/2019035069
LC ebook record available at https://lccn.loc.gov/2019035070

Printed in China
(hc) 10 9 8 7 6 5 4 3 2 1

Illustrations done in mixed media then painted digitally
Display type set in FloraDora by Nick Curtis
Text type set in Visby Round by Connary Fagen
Color separations by Colourscan Print Co Pte Ltd, Singapore
Printed by 1010 Printing International Limited in Huizhou, Guangdong, China
Production supervision by Jennifer Most Delaney

Shhh!
The Baby's Asleep

JaNay Brown-Wood   Illustrated by **Elissambura**

ini **Charlesbridge**

Now don't make a peep. . . .
The baby's finally asleep.

Mom creeps to the door
and hears sounds from the floor.

"Shhh! The baby's asleep!"

CREAK!

CREAK!

CREAK!

Daddy's loud belly wants PB and jelly.

GRUMBLE!

GRUMBLE!
GRUMBLE!
GRUMBLE!

"Shhh! The baby's asleep!"

Grammy's new shirt
is covered in dirt.

"*Shhh!* The baby's asleep!"

Pop Pop's red nose
just needs some good blows.

"Shhh! The baby's asleep!"

WHIR!

WHIR!

Shae's hair is still wet;
her curls haven't set.

BANG

BANG

BANG

BAN

Dante's toy truck
needs its wheels unstuck.

"*Shhh! The baby's asleep!*"

Rover's big jowls
are due for some howls.

"Shhh! The baby's asleep!"

And what's that? Oh no!
Mr. Young starts to mow!

"Shhhhhhhhhh!
The baby's asleep!"

WWAAAAAAAAA

All these uproars
while the poor baby snores.
Now the baby's awake—
for goodness' sake!

You know what we need?
A good book to read!

Now don't make a peep . . .

CLICK!

. . . so the family can sleep!